GW00865338

About the Author

D. Devereoux was born in St. Louis, Missouri, but spent most his adult life in San Diego, California. He began keeping a journal at the age of nineteen. Throughout his journey of self-discovery, he would look back on his journal entries and he could see valuable experiences and life lessons he had learned. Devereoux has taken those experiences and formulated stories based around the many lessons he has learned. He hopes his stories will touch and inspire people to keep a journal and reflect on their unique and incredible lives.

The Cautionary Tale of Mr. Oliver Owl and Ruben Rabbit

D. Devereoux

Illustrations by Katarzyna Maciak

The Cautionary Tale of Mr. Oliver Owl and Ruben Rabbit

Olympia Publishers
London

www.olympiapublishers.com
OLYMPIA PAPERBACK EDITION

Copyright © D. Devereoux 2020
Illustrations by Katarzyna Maciak
The right of D. Devereoux to be identified as author of
this work has been asserted in accordance with sections 77 and 78
of the Copyright, Designs and Patents Act 1988.

All Rights Reserved

No reproduction, copy or transmission of this publication
may be made without written permission.
No paragraph of this publication may be reproduced,
copied or transmitted save with the written permission of the
publisher, or in accordance with the provisions
of the Copyright Act 1956 (as amended).

Any person who commits any unauthorised act in relation to
this publication may be liable to criminal
prosecution and civil claims for damage.

A CIP catalogue record for this title is
available from the British Library.

ISBN: 978-1-78830-311-8

This is a work of fiction.
Names, characters, places and incidents originate from the writer's
imagination. Any resemblance to actual persons, living or dead, is
purely coincidental.

First Published in 2020

Olympia Publishers
60 Cannon Street
London
EC4N 6NP

Printed in Great Britain

Dedication

The book is dedicated to my grandmother, mother, aunts, dad, sisters, brothers, cousins, nieces, nephews, godmother, godchildren and my friends.

Acknowledgements

I would like to thank the matriarchs in my family to help inspire this children's fable. I would also like to acknowledge my friend, Gallin Chappell, for bringing my story to life with his early illustrations. I would also like to acknowledge my godsister, Debra, who inspired me to keep a journal and become a writer. Recording a journal has been the greatest therapeutic tool to reflect and grow into a mature human being and for that I am forever grateful.

Our Story begins with Ruben Rabbit venturing into
Nefarious Forest for the very first time and comes
across Mr. Oliver Owl in a big oak tree at the entrance
of the forest.

Hi, my name is Ruben Rabbit.

Hi Ruben, my name is Mr. Oliver Owl.

Ruben ask Mr. Oliver, "Will you be my friend?"

Mr. Oliver says, "Yes, Ruben I'll be your friend till the
end."

Ruben says, "I'm thinking about exploring Nefarious
Forest, Mr. Oliver."

Mr. Oliver says, "Stay alert Ruben, the forest is
dangerous and there are lots of predators that will eat
you. The forest has many hidden and unhidden dangers

"Beware of the dangers above."

"Beware of the dangers below."

Beware of the dangers in front"

Beware of the dangers behind.

"Mr. Oliver, I'm quicker and faster than anything."
Mr. Oliver says, "Be cautious Ruben Rabbit, keep your
eyes open. Remember Ruben you can't see all the
predators."

As Ruben enters Nefarious Forest a hawk swoops down out of the sky to eat Ruben.

Ruben runs as fast as fast as he can and escapes the hawk.

Ruben returns to Mr. Oliver.
"Mr. Oliver, Mr. Oliver what was that? What was that?"
"That was a hawk Ruben, the danger from above."
"I told you Mr. Oliver I'm quicker and faster than
anything."

Ruben goes to the river to get a drink of water.

A crocodile jumps out of the river to eat Ruben.
Ruben runs as fast as fast as he can and escapes the
crocodile.

Ruben returns to Mr. Oliver.
"Mr. Oliver, Mr. Oliver what was that? What was that?"
"That was a crocodile Ruben, the danger from below."
"I told you Mr. Oliver, I'm quicker and faster than
anything."

Ruben goes further into the forest to explore.

A snake sneaks up behind to eat Ruben.
Ruben runs as fast as fast as he can and escape the
snake.

Ruben returns to Mr. Oliver.
"Mr. Oliver, Mr. Oliver what was that? What was that?"
"That was a snake Ruben, the danger from behind."
"I told you Mr. Oliver I'm quicker and faster than
anything."

Ruben continues further into the forest.
He comes across a pack wolves ahead.

Ruben runs as fast as fast as he can, faster than he has ever ran before in every direction and manages to narrowly escape through a rabbit hole.

"Mr. Oliver, Mr. Oliver what was that? What was that?"
"That was a pack of wolves Ruben the danger ahead."
"See Mr. Oliver I told you I'm quicker and faster than
anything, even a pack of wolves."

"Ruben, you really are fast. No one hardly ever escapes
the pack of wolves."
In an instant Mr. Oliver swoops down on Ruben.

Ruben never suspected Mr. Oliver Owl was the most
dangerous predator of them all.

What do you think happened to Ruben?